COSMIC COLIN

Ticking Time Bomb

BUSTER

CHAPTER ONE

We'd just left school when Harry's space communicator beeped. He glanced at it and gasped.

What is it?

Nothing important. But I've got to go now because I've got a tummy ache. If you never see me again, it's because I died from it. Bye!

Harry tried to run away, but I grabbed his arm.

You just got a distress call, didn't you? Don't think you can sneak off and have an adventure without me.

This time I can't let you come. It will be far too dangerous.

At least tell me what it's all about.

The most evil man in the universe has escaped from prison. His name is Galactic Gary, and he's planning to destroy time itself. I need to face him, and I need to do it alone.

I wanted to let Harry go off on his own,
but I just couldn't do it.

I don't care how dangerous it is. I can't stay behind.

Okay. But don't say I didn't warn you.

So where are we going?

The headquarters of the intergalactic police. The place Galactic Gary escaped from. They'll explain our mission when we get there.

I followed Harry to his spacebin, a bin that can take us ...

ANYWHERE IN TIME AND SPACE

... and I'm usually really excited about getting in. But this time was different. It all felt much more serious.

CHAPTER TWO

The police space station was a huge
floating ring of offices, courtrooms and
prisons. Outside the large, curved windows
I could see shuttles flying off with their
blue lights flashing.

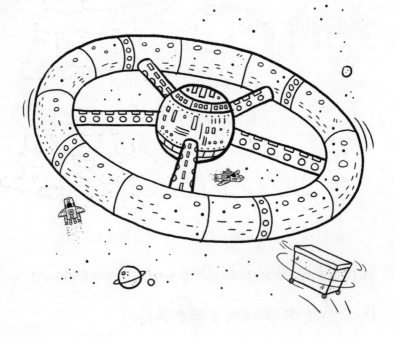

Two policemen greeted us and led us down
the corridor into a small office.

Inside, a policeman wearing dark glasses was sitting behind a desk.

Thanks so much for answering my call, Harry. My name is Officer Stern and I'm looking after the case.

What happened? How did Galactic Gary escape?

No one is sure. We found his cell empty a few days ago. He left a note inside.

One of the policemen stepped forward and handed us a scrap of paper.

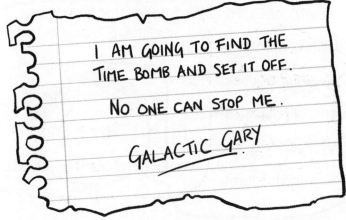

I AM GOING TO FIND THE TIME BOMB AND SET IT OFF.

NO ONE CAN STOP ME.

GALACTIC GARY

That's not possible! He can't know where it is.

What's a time bomb?

It's the most dangerous weapon ever created. It could explode time itself, meaning that yesterday becomes tomorrow and next Wednesday becomes last Friday.

That's terrible. Weekends could disappear altogether and life would be unbearable.

It's so dangerous it was split into three parts by the intergalactic police. The parts were stored on three different planets, and I'm one of the only people who knows where they are. Galactic Gary must have somehow tracked them down.

THE TIME BOMB

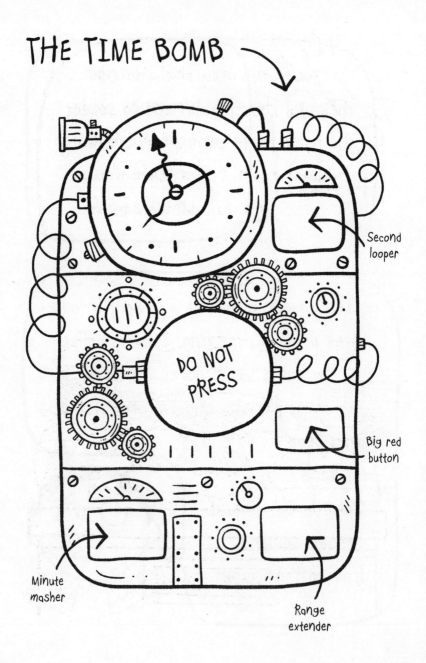

Second looper

DO NOT PRESS

Big red button

Minute masher

Range extender

Stay right here, Officer Stern. I'll set my time co-ordinates so we arrive back just one minute from now. If you don't see us again very soon, it means we failed our mission.

You can do it, Harry. We're all counting on you.

We headed back to the spacebin.

That doesn't sound too bad, does it? We've just got to pop to three planets and pick up some bomb parts.

You don't understand. The space police didn't just hide the bomb on ordinary planets. They chose the places no one would ever think of looking. We've got to visit three of the weirdest places in the universe.

CHAPTER THREE

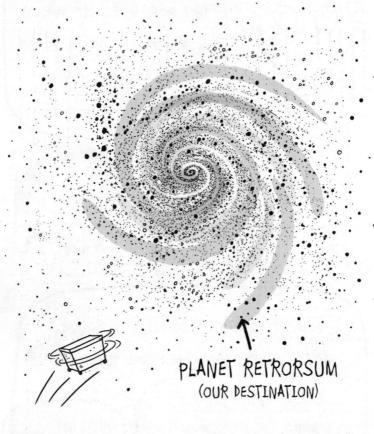

PLANET RETRORSUM
(OUR DESTINATION)

We jumped into the spacebin and Harry
set the controls for a distant corner
of the pinwheel Galaxy.

We landed on a busy street lined with tall office blocks and busy shops.

We peered inside a large office building.

Men and women wearing smart clothes were sitting in front of laptops.

A small child walked in and planted his hands on his hips.

I hope you're all doing well with your spreadsheets, because anyone who doesn't get theirs done by the end of the day will get detention.

What?

Everyone else gets ages to do theirs.

That's so unfair.

What's wrong with those people?

On this planet everyone is born as adults and they get younger as time passes. This means the adults act like children and the children act like adults.

That sounds pretty confusing.

It is. But we might be able to use the strangeness of this place to our advantage. We've got to recover the first part of the bomb from the Secret Service Headquarters, and I think I know how to do it.

I tried to focus on our mission, but I couldn't take my eyes off all the odd things around us.

29

CHAPTER FOUR

We arrived at the Secret Service HQ to find two guards standing by the front door.

33

We found ourselves in a large office filled with the Secret Service workers.

We need to get to that treasure room at the back of the office. Watch this ...

HEY EVERYONE! WHO WANTS TO PLAY HIDE AND SEEK? I'LL BE 'IT'.

Harry covered his eyes and counted to ten, and the office workers ducked under their desks.

We strolled right past them and into the treasure room.

I rifled through large stacks of jewels
and golden coins, but there was no
sign of the bomb.

I was on my third shelf when I heard the
door open.

Oh no! Do you think
Galactic Gary has
caught up with
us already?

A small child burst in.

What are you doing in here? How did you get past my staff?

I'm sorry we had to sneak in, but this is really important. We're trying to save the entire universe.

Get away from my treasure!

He seemed angry, but I didn't see what harm he could do. He was only a weak toddler, after all.

Then he pulled out a sonic blasterizer.
UH-OH.

I ran along the side of the room and the
boy chased after me. This meant Harry
could keep looking for the bomb, but it
also meant I was in the line of fire.

The boy fired, but I managed to leap
away in time. The wall behind me
exploded in huge chunks.

Harry was shouting from the other side of the room.

Stay close to the shelves. He won't fire at them in case he damages the treasure.

I pressed myself against one of the
shelves. The toddler stamped his feet
on the floor.

> Thieves! You won't
> get away with this.

Harry was right. For all his yelling, the boy
wouldn't fire at any of his precious stuff.

I shuffled along the shelf, keeping my back to the treasure and my eye on the toddler.

When I reached the end I could see Harry. He was just a few rows away, standing inside the spacebin and holding the lid open. I'd have to move away from the treasure to get to him, giving the boy a chance to shoot.

I forced myself to go. I heard the low pulse of the blasterizer as soon as I started running. A ball of blinding white light hurtled towards me.

I felt the heat blast the back of my head as I ran. It must have missed me by inches.

I clambered into the spacebin and
yanked the lid shut, while Harry
slammed the controls.

We were gone before the toddler
could fire again.

CHAPTER FIVE

Our next stop was in the Cartwheel Galaxy.

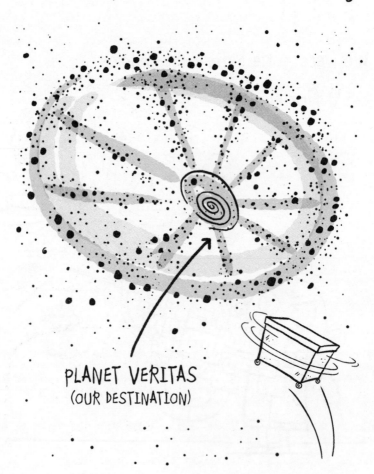

PLANET VERITAS
(OUR DESTINATION)

The next piece is stored in the
secret section of this city's museum.
I don't know exactly where that is,
but I'm sure the locals will help.

This planet looked pretty normal
at first, too.

Excuse me, do you know the way to the museum?

Yes, but I can't be bothered to help you.

Excuse me, do you know the way to the museum?

No, but I wear the same underpants for days on end.

What's going on?

No one on this planet can lie. The gravity affects their brains and makes it impossible.

Well that shouldn't be a problem for me because I sometimes lie.

I realised what I'd just said. I'd told my
mouth to say, "Well that shouldn't be a
problem for me because I never lie." But
the words changed as I said them.

It seemed as though everyone on the
planet had to be honest all the time,
even us.

As Harry went off to get help, I looked around the strange, honest world.

PRICEY CLOTHES

DON'T BUY ANYTHING YET, OUR SALE STARTS NEXT WEEK

PETS WITH STINKY BREATH!

Finally, Harry found someone who could help us.

It's two miles down this road. I'm going that way myself, but I'm not going to offer you a lift because I've just farted in my car.

We arrived at the museum half an hour later.

CHAPTER SIX

The door to the secret section was at the back of the main hall. There was a guard standing next to it.

TOP
SECRET

PASSES MUST
BE SHOWN

Okay, here's the plan. We pretend to be inspectors and say we need to check that the shelves are sturdy enough.

Great idea. If he asks to see our passes, I'll say we left them in our car.

We approached the guard.

I'm sorry but I can't let you in without a pass.

We're not inspectors and we don't have to check your shelves.

We went back up to the guard.

Please can you let us in? We want to steal something from the secret section. It's part of a time bomb that we're keeping away from an evil villain called Galactic Gary. He wants to destroy time itself. That will harm every planet, including yours.

That does all sound very serious. But I'm still not going to let you in, just to make myself feel important.

Give us a chance to change your mind. I have a bin that can take us anywhere in space and time. We could visit some of the best places in the universe, so you'll see the amazing things you'll be helping to save. I'll make sure we return just after we leave, so you won't have to abandon your post. What do you say?

Okay. I don't see why not.

Harry summoned the spacebin and
we all got in.

We visited the bouncy planet of Centauri.

We went to the Ursa Major carnival, the biggest party in the universe.

And we watched a triple sunset in the Andromeda Galaxy.

After the three suns had sunk below the horizon, we wandered back to the spacebin.

Now that you've seen how awesome the universe is, will you help us save it?

Sorry but no. This has been fun, but my duty is still more important to me than anything else.

I understand. In that case, I'll take you back to your planet and we'll give up on our quest.

We landed outside the museum and the
guard went back in.

So that's it? We're
just going to give up
on our quest and let
Galactic Gary destroy
time itself?

Of course not. I was
lying to the guard, which
is why I had to say it
before we came back to this
planet. Halfway through the
carnival parade, I slipped
back here in the spacebin
and grabbed the second
part of the bomb.

Won't the guard get upset when he finds out?

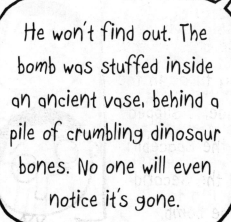

He won't find out. The bomb was stuffed inside an ancient vase, behind a pile of crumbling dinosaur bones. No one will even notice it's gone.

Great, so just one more part to get now. We're almost there.

Not quite. The final bit of our mission will be the toughest of all. It's on one of the most dangerous planets in the world, and we're almost certainly going to die.

WHAT?

Whoops. I should probably have waited until we were off the truth planet before telling you about it.

CHAPTER SEVEN

PLANET ANIMALUS
HORRIBILIS
(OUR DESTINATION)

Our final stop was on the edge of the
Whirlpool Galaxy.

No wonder Harry warned me about this place. The street was filled with snakes, crocodiles and scorpions.

How will we get past all these dangerous beasts?

Actually, these ones are harmless. On this planet, animals like snakes and scorpions are all perfectly safe.

Harry went up to a cobra that was
perched on a garden wall. He stroked
it and it purred.

I carefully reached out for the snake.
Instead of lashing out and biting me,
it nuzzled my hand.

I felt something brush against my leg
and looked down to see a giant tarantula.

I flinched back, but it just grinned and
yapped adorably.

Everywhere I looked, I could see fearsome beasts being treated like pampered pets.

In a park across the street, a woman was throwing a stick for her crocodile to fetch.

A grizzly bear stuck its head out of
a passing car and smiled at me.

A couple strolled past with a baby in a
pram. Instead of a dolly, it was hugging
a live scorpion.

What's so bad about this planet, then?

Just as animals that are deadly on Earth are cute here, animals that are cute in your world are deadly here.

Okay ...

The final part of the bomb is stored in a closed-down library. Apparently, it's now infested with ... KITTENS!

Oh. I see.

WAAAH!

I tried my best to look frightened.

It wasn't very convincing. All we had to
do was wander into an old library and
steal a bomb from some kittens. How
hard could it be?

I'm sure they were very vicious as kittens
went, but they were still only kittens.

This seemed like it was going to be
the easiest part of the mission,
not the hardest.

CHAPTER EIGHT

The old library was on the edge of a park in a deserted part of town.

There was a battered wooden door at the top of some wide stone steps. Harry glanced at some tiny claw marks and winced.

We entered the dark building and Harry shone the light of his space communicator ahead.

We were in a long corridor with a weird tangy smell. It took a moment for me to recognise it as cat wee.

A soft mewing echoed ahead of us. Harry's hands trembled, making the light wobble.

I think there might be a kitten in here. I know it's difficult, but we must go on. The entire universe is depending on us.

I'm sure we'll be fine.

It was great to be the brave one for once.

I could see Harry was frightened, but I

couldn't really understand why.

Harry gasped and pointed to a dark shape

that was strolling towards us.

It was a small grey kitten. I crouched down
and clicked my fingers.

Here, kitty kitty.

The kitten pounced on my chest and
almost knocked me to the floor.

The kitten climbed up to my neck and
drew back its right paw.

It slapped me over and over again.

I tried to wrestle the beast away, but it was too strong.

Harry managed to wrench the creature free.

He flung it down the corridor and we
raced away.

I could hear the tiny beast scampering behind us. We had to get away before it struck again.

We hurtled through a door into a large, murky room. I slammed it shut, shoved a bolt across and watched in horror as tiny dents appeared in the wood.

The kitten was flinging itself against the other side.

That door won't hold for much longer. We need to find the last part of the bomb and summon the spacebin right now.

We were inside the main room of the library. Rows of high shelves surrounded us. Some were empty, while others were stacked with mouldy books.

Harry shone his light around the rotten bookcases, but there was no sign of the time bomb.

Something was stirring on top of one
of the shelves. It leapt down at me.

phew! It was just a snake. The poor thing
must have got trapped inside the library
by mistake.

I opened a window and let it slither out.
I really hoped it could get safely back
to its owners.

I've found it!

Harry rushed towards a broken display case at the far end of the room. The last part of the bomb was propped up on the middle shelf.

Something was glinting above it. In the light of Harry's space communicator, I could make out two pairs of tiny blue eyes.

The fiends pounced on Harry, clamping
on to his shoulders and legs.

I ran over and ripped one of the kittens from Harry's back. A large strip of his shirt came away with it.

The beast whipped its head round and sank its sharp teeth into my hand.

I shrieked and let go.

I needed a way to distract the killer kitties.

I thought about my Aunt Sarah's cat Frodo. He loves chasing balls of string. If I could find some, I could distract the beasts for long enough to grab the bomb.

I spotted a small cupboard in the corner and dashed over to it.

Inside were shelves lined with cleaning products. There was no string, but there was something even better.

There was a large hoover at the bottom
of the cupboard.

I remembered how Frodo would flee for the
curtains whenever Aunt Sarah used hers.

If it had the same effect on these kittens,
they might leave us alone for long enough
to get the bomb.

I plugged the hoover in and flicked the
switch on the side. It spluttered on.

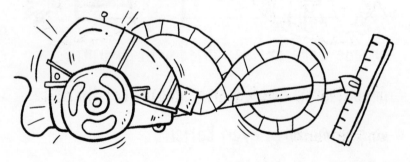

The kittens yowled and darted for the edge
of the room.

I rushed over to the display case. I thought I heard something clatter to the ground as I took the bomb, but there was no time to check.

I clutched the bomb to my chest and jumped
into the bin.

CHAPTER NINE

We plonked the bomb parts on Officer Stern's desk. We were sweating, we were out of breath and our clothes had been shredded by the kittens.

I can see that you boys went through hell to bring this bomb to us and I can't thank you enough. No one else could have done it.

Officer Stern laid the three parts out in front of him and fiddled with them.

So how are we going to destroy it?

I'll get to that in a minute. But first, I need to check it's all here.

The police officer was fixing the different bits of the bomb together. It seemed a dangerous way to check it.

Officer Stern continued connecting
the wires.

Oh, I'll set it off alright. But it won't be an accident.

Officer Stern whipped off his hat and dark glasses and peeled off his moustache. Then he placed a large blue space helmet over his head.

Of course, it was me all along. I can't believe you fell for it. But thanks for bringing me the bomb. Like I said, no one else could have done it.

I turned to the policemen behind Galactic Gary.

Arrest him! He's an imposter.

But the policemen just backed into the corners and cowered.

I've waited so long for this. Finally, I shall destroy TIME itself.

Galactic Gary clutched the bomb to his chest and stood up.

Gary pressed the button on the front of the bomb.

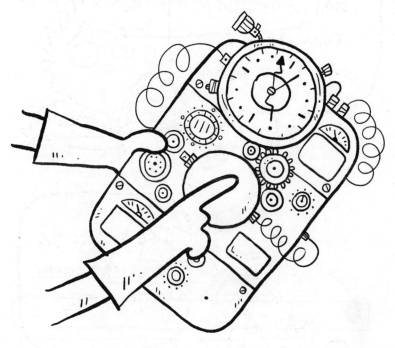

We ducked down and braced ourselves. I wasn't really sure how this would protect against time exploding, but I felt I had to do something.

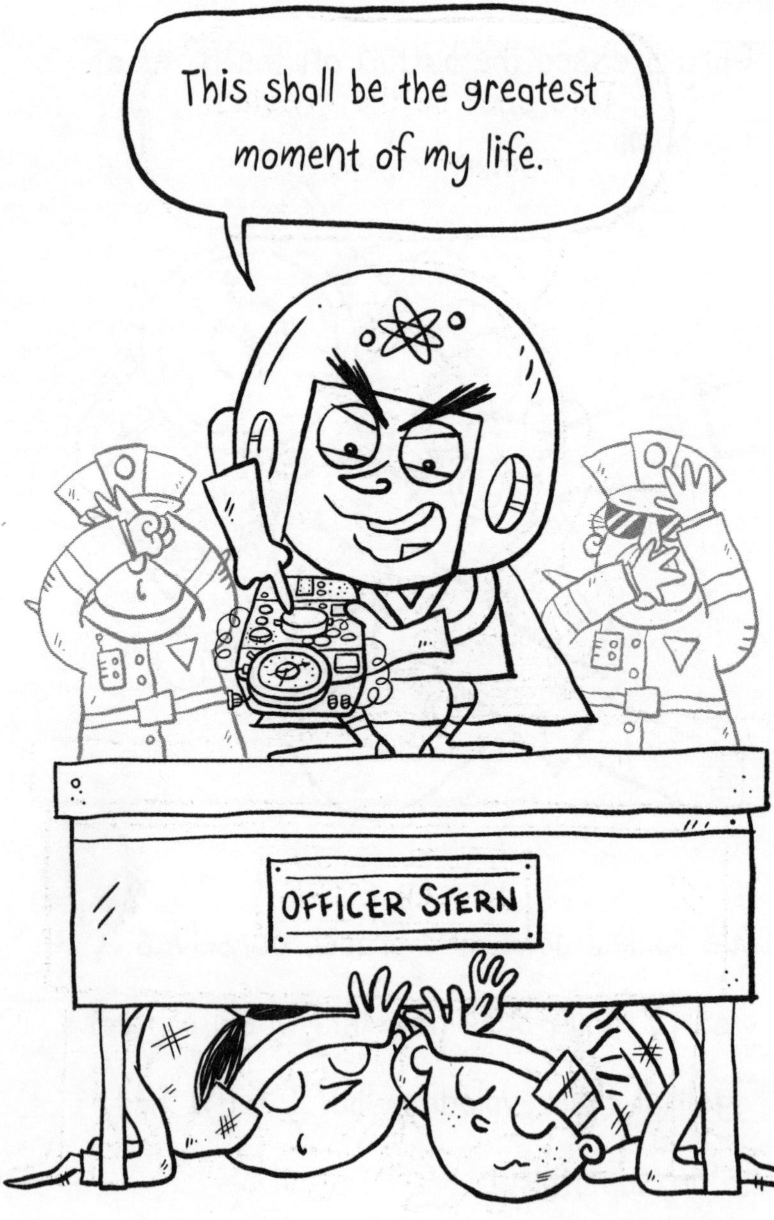
This shall be the greatest moment of my life.
OFFICER STERN

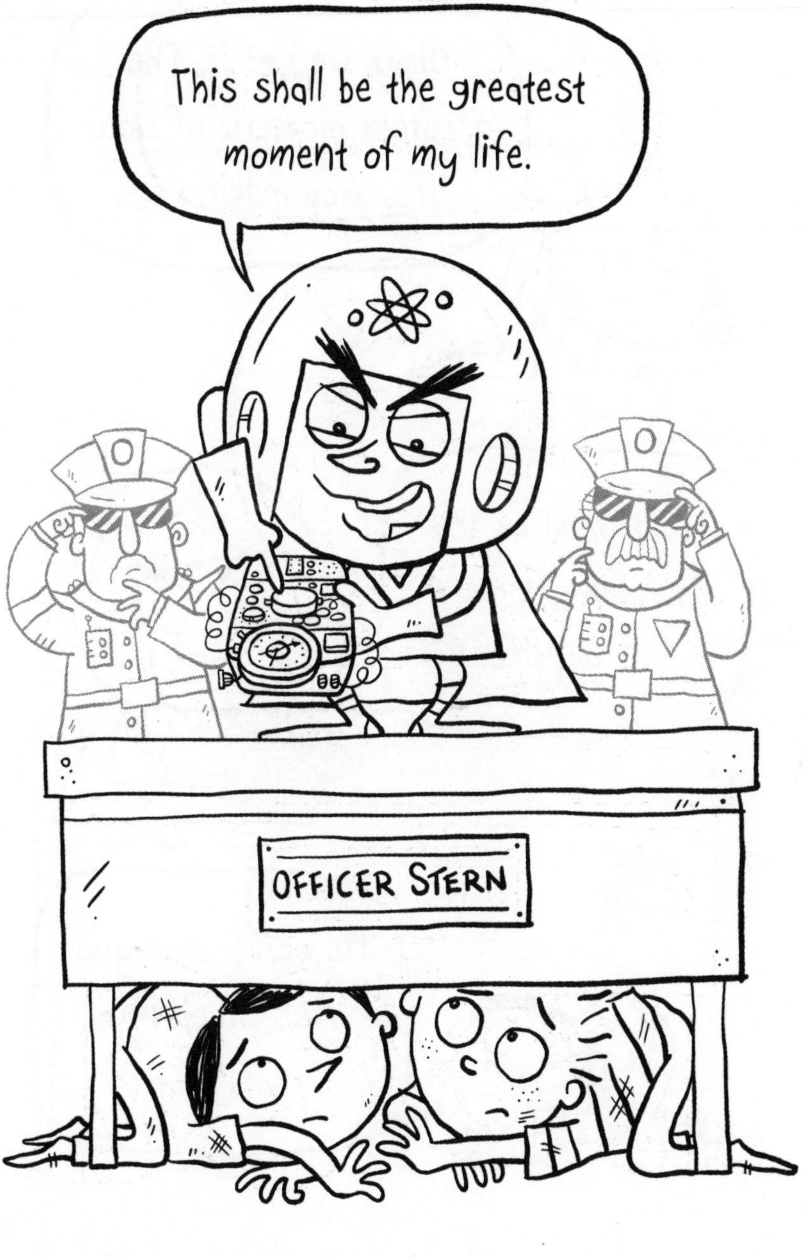
This shall be the greatest moment of my life.
OFFICER STERN

Galactic Gary kept repeating the same words and pressing the big red button over and over again. The policemen stepped forward and grabbed his arms.

I'm arresting you on a charge of pretending to be a police officer and trying to destroy time itself.

This shall be the greatest moment of my life.

I don't understand. We collected all the parts. The bomb should have worked.

I thought back to our mad scramble away from the kittens.

I heard something fall on to the floor when I grabbed the last part of the bomb. Maybe it was an important bit.

Of course, look! The range extender is missing. So when Gary pressed the button, it only worked on him, trapping him in a time loop.

So I saved the whole universe just by accidentally dropping a bit of the bomb?

Even better. You also trapped Galactic Gary in a time loop forever. He'll never be able to break out of prison again.

The policemen marched Galactic Gary back to his cell.

We jumped back in the spacebin and went home, knowing that time and space were safe from Galactic Gary once again.

Grab your copy of Cosmic Colin's third adventure!

Out now!